March 31, 2002

Dearest Christopher,

Happy Easter! You are such a great boy who grows bigger every day. Mommy and Daddy are so proud of you. We hope you enjoy the Easter egg hunt the bunny left for you.

We love you so,
Mommy & Daddy
xo xo
xo

This book belongs to

Christopher Peck

W9-CHN-056

Tips for Reading and Sharing

Are You Spring? is a gentle story about a funny misunderstanding – the kind that children will recognize and laugh at. They will also identify with Una's burning curiosity for an answer to her question.

Read on to find out how to get the most fun out of this story.

Zzzzzzzz   Zzzzzzz

GROWL!

Be a bear!

Snuggle up like Big Bear Mother and her cubs and have a good time with this book. Your child will love to join in with the noises in the story. *Snoooore* like sleeping bears; GROWL! to scare away the wolves; and *buzzzzzz* like bees doing their honey dance.

Now join in!

Let your child turn the pages. Point to the words as you read and encourage him to join in. The rhythm of the opening lines makes them especially fun to say. He will also want to call out repeated phrases like *"Are you Spring?"* Remembering a few key words or phrases like this one will really boost his confidence.

What season is it?

This story introduces the difficult concept of changing seasons. Talk with your child about weather and the seasons. Ask him what he likes best about each season. Talk about Una's feelings as she tries to be independent – feelings that your child will also be experiencing.

Picture clues – can you spy the rabbit?

Ask your child to look at the pictures for clues that winter is turning to spring. Notice how the colors change. What happens to the rabbit? Look at the animals – how do they survive in the cold? You might even talk about why bears hibernate. Don't worry if, like Una, your child doesn't quite understand.

Have a good time and enjoy the magic of the story!

Bernice E. Cullinan

Bernice E. Cullinan
Reading Consultant

For Barbara Buckley, who loved the spring – C.P.
Help save the bears! Write to *The Raincoast Conservation Society, P. O. Box 26,*
Bella Bella, British Columbia V0T 1B0, Canada; ikrcoast@islandnet.com – C.W.

Dorling Kindersley Publishing, Inc.

95 Madison Avenue
New York, New York 10016

Text copyright © 2000 by Caroline Pitcher
Illustrations copyright © 2000 by Cliff Wright

Library of Congress Cataloging-in-Publication Data

Pitcher, Caroline.

Are you spring? / by Caroline Pitcher. – 1st American ed.

p. cm. – (Share-a-story)

Summary: After being told that she cannot leave her winter den until spring arrives, Una the bear cub
goes out early, meets various animals, gets in trouble, and eventually finds out what spring is.

ISBN 0-7894-6350-4 (hardcover)
ISBN 0-7894-5614-1 (paperback)

[1. Bears–Fiction. 2. Animals–Fiction. 3. Spring–Fiction.] I. Title. II. Share-a-story (DK Publishing, Inc.)

PZ7.P6427 Ar 2000 [E]–dc21   99-049804

Color reproduction by Dot Gradations, UK
Printed in Hong Kong by Wing King Tong

First American Edition, 2000

2 4 6 8 10 9 7 5 3 1

Published in Great Britain by Dorling Kindersley Limited.

Acknowledgments:
Series Reading Consultant: Wendy Cooling   **Series Activities Advisor:** Lianna Hodson
Photographer: Steve Gorton   **Models:** Sami, Anisa, and Aziz Khan, Ryan Heaton
U.S. Consultant: Bernice E. Cullinan, Professor of Reading, New York University

For our complete
catalog visit
www.dk.com

Are You Spring?

Caroline Pitcher • *Cliff Wright*

Dorling Kindersley Publishing, Inc.

Deep in the forest was the brown bears' den.
Deep in the den two cubs were born.
They slept and ate and ate and slept.

One day the she-cub sat up and said, "I want to go out there."

Big Bear Mother shook her head and said, "It's Winter, Una. Now go back to sleep like your good little brother."

Una scowled at her brother and said, "But when can I go out there?"

"When Spring comes," grunted Big Bear Mother.

So Una snuggled up and fell asleep wondering who Spring was.

A few days later Una woke up again.
She padded across the den and looked outside.

The snow dazzled her new little eyes.
"Shall I tell Spring to hurry up?" she called.
But Big Bear Mother didn't answer.
She was fast asleep, snoring.
Una was curious. She scampered
out of the den . . .

And into the forest.

She saw a funny tree with two brown knobbly branches.

"Are you Spring?" she asked. "You've got big clumsy feet!"

"Those are my snowshoes," laughed Moose. "And I'm not Spring. But Spring is in the air when the trees sprout fresh leaves."

Una gazed up at the bright new leaves.

Tock-tock-tock, tock-tock-tock said someone up above.

"Are you Spring?" asked Una.

"No," said Woodpecker. "But Spring is coming when woodpeckers drum and birds build their nests."

Suddenly someone jumped out from behind a tree.

"Are you Spring?" cried Una. "You've got such sharp teeth."

"No," said Little Wolf. "I'm a cub."

"No, you're not!" said Una. "I'm a cub and so is my brother, so I know what they look like!"

"You're a bear cub. I'm a wolf cub," explained Little Wolf.

A dark shadow fell across the snow.

Una looked up. There was another wolf cub, but twenty times bigger. "If you're Spring," she whispered, "I don't think I like you."

Then a voice Una knew
growled, "Una! Quickly!
Climb that tree!"

And Una found she could climb, quickly!
Big Bear Mother reared up and roared and
scared the wolves away.

Then she cried, "Una! Where have you been?
I woke up and you were gone!"

"Mom! I was so frightened on my own!
I was only looking for Spring. . . ."

Big Bear Mother nuzzled Una and said,
"Spring will be here soon, but now it's time
to go home."

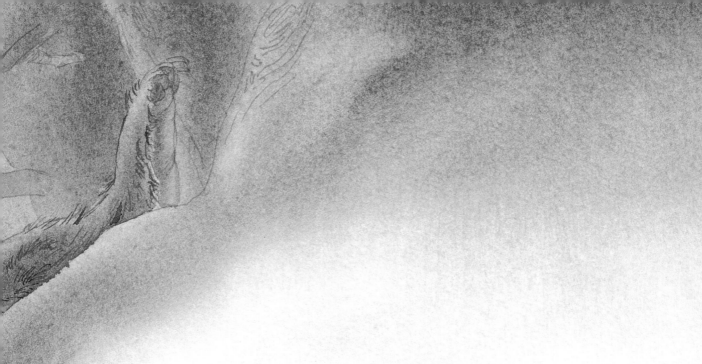

Back in the den, the bears cuddled in a cozy heap. Big Bear Mother said, "Snuggle up and listen to me, my cubs, and I will tell you stories of Spring."

Una and her brother snuggled up closer.

"Now, when Spring comes, the great snows melt. Rivers run fast. The fish leap high above the rocks, and I will teach you how to catch them. . . ."

"Green leaves sprout on trees, wildflowers open in the grass, and blueberries swell, so juicy and purple, especially for bears to eat."

Big Bear Mother licked her lips.

"And, best of all, the bees buzz, doing their honey dance, up and down, around and around, leading us to their golden honey."

"Yummy!" cried Una, rolling and tumbling around the den. She couldn't wait for Spring to come!

So, night after night, snug inside their den, the cubs listened to Big Bear Mother's tales. Until Una couldn't wait any longer. "But who is Spring?" she cried. "And when will she come?"

Big Bear Mother laughed. She padded to the entrance of the den and looked out.

"This is Spring, Una!
Come and see her now.
She's here!"

Activities to Enjoy

I f you've enjoyed this story, you might like to try some of these simple, fun activities with your child.

What's it like outside?

Look in magazines for pictures of the seasons. Point out clues that indicate the season, such as golden leaves in fall. Ask your child to draw pictures of spring, summer, fall, and winter, including his favorite things to do in each season. Write a simple descriptive sentence on each picture, then staple the pages together to make a book.

Cozy bear den

Your child can easily make a bear den by draping a sheet or blanket over some chairs or a table. Children will enjoy pretending to be Una sleeping in the den or exploring the forest. What would Una eat? What games would she play?

What's the weather?

Play a dress-up game! Ask your child to put on the special clothes that he wears in the sun, snow, and rain.

Sprout seeds!

In the story, Moose tells Una, "*Spring is in the air when the trees sprout fresh leaves.*" Have fun sprouting some shoots of your own.

What you will need: Paints or felt-tip pens; egg shells; cotton balls; a lima bean or some watercress seeds; water.

Draw or paint faces on the broken egg shells. Keep them steady in an egg carton. Next, place wet cotton balls in the egg shells.

Put a lima bean or some watercress seeds on the cotton balls. Finally, place your egg shells on a window sill and keep the cotton balls moist.

Wait and watch as your faces grow green hair!

Other Share-a-Story titles to collect:

Not Now, Mrs. Wolf!
by Shen Roddie
illustrated by Selina Young

The Caterpillar That Roared
by Michael Lawrence
illustrated by Alison Bartlett

Neil's Numberless World
by Lucy Coats
illustrated by Neal Layton